THE CHILDREN'S HOUSE
OF BUCKS COUNTY
840 TRENTON RD.
FAIRLESS HILLS, PA. 19030
215-943-3656
NURSERY SCHOOL & KINDERGARTEN

The ANIMALS' SONG

by David L. Harrison

Illustrated by Chris L. Demarest

Boyds Mills Press

To Tyler and Kristopher with
grandfatherly love
—D. L. H.

To the
Tuesday morning playgroup
—C. L. D.

There was a girl
With a silver flute,
Toot toot
Tootity toot,
Who puckered her lips
And blew her flute,
Tootity tootity toot.

She met a boy
With a rumity drum,
Rum tum
Rumity tum,
Who joined the girl
And played his drum,
Rumity tumity tum.

A hooty owl
Heard the flute,
Hoot hoot
Hootity hoot.
He winked at the drum
And blinked at the flute,
Hootity hootity hoot.

A sleepy dog
Taking a nap,
Yip yap
Yippity yap,
Joined the band
And left his nap,
Yippity yippity yap.

A gentle cow
With grass to chew,
Moo moo
Moodily moo,
Swished her tail
And the rest of her, too,
Moodily moodily moo.

Prancing pony,
Dappledy gray,
Neigh neigh
Neighdity neigh,
Jumped the fence
And ran away,
Neighdity neighdity neigh.

Rooster crowed
And flapped and flew,
Cock-a-doodle
Doodily do,
To join the band
He flapped and flew,
Cock-a-doodily do.

They danced and sang,
Tootity toot,
Rumity tum,
Hootity hoot.

Yippity yap,
Moodily moo,
Neighdity neigh,
Doodily do.

A bowlegged pig,
Chubby and short,
Snort snort
Snortity snort,
Grunted a squeal
And squealed a snort,
Snortity snortity snort.

A bird with a cherry
Ready to eat,
Tweet tweet
Tweetity tweet,
Sang to the flute
With song so sweet,
Tweetity tweetity tweet.

Cranky old goose
Who honked and hissed,
Honk honk
Hissity hiss,
Stretched her neck
And looked like this!
Hissity hissity hiss.

The lamb who leaped
On nimble feet,
Bleat bleat
Bleatity bleat,
Heard the drum
And felt the beat,
Bleatity bleatity bleat.

A swimming duck
With a shiny back,
Quack quack
Quackity quack,
Swam away
But swam right back,
Quackity quackity quack.

The pigeon cooed,
As pigeons do,
Coo coo
Cooity coo.
She left the barn
And away she flew,
Cooity cooity coo.

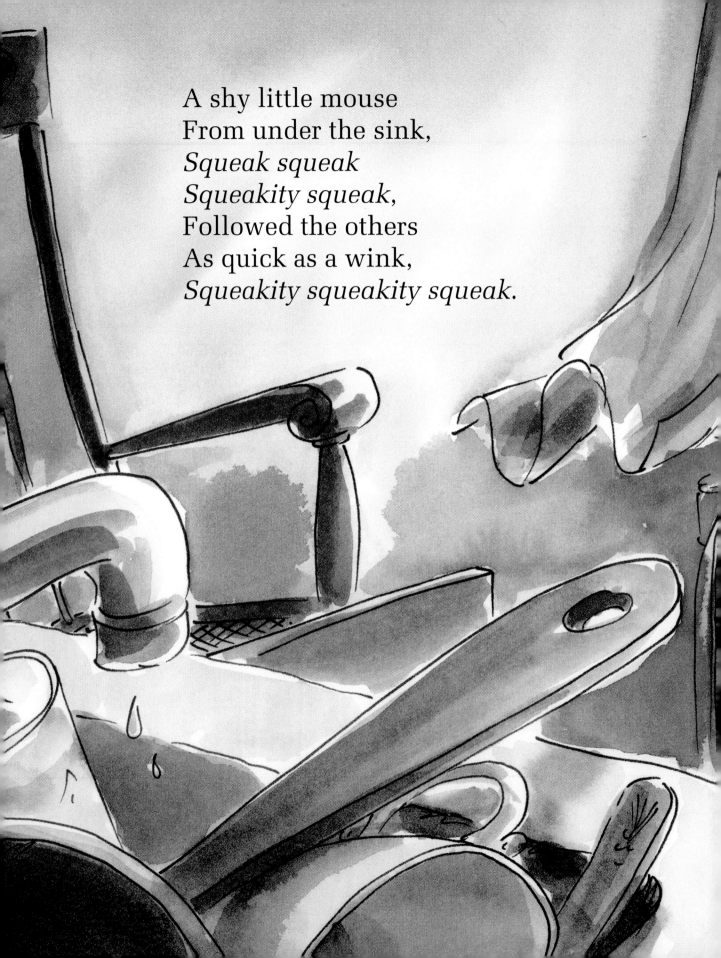

A shy little mouse
From under the sink,
Squeak squeak
Squeakity squeak,
Followed the others
As quick as a wink,
Squeakity squeakity squeak.

They danced and sang,
Tootity toot,
Rumity tum,
Hootity hoot...

Yippity yap,
Moodily moo,
Neighdity neigh,
Doodily do. . .

Snortity snort,
Tweetity tweet,
Hissity hiss,
Bleatity bleat. . .

Quackity quack,
Cooity coo,
Squeakity squeak
The whole day through.

They sang and danced
And skipped along
With a flute and a drum
And the animals' song.

Text copyright © 1997 by David L. Harrison
Illustrations copyright © 1997 by Chris L. Demarest
All rights reserved

Published by Caroline House
Boyds Mills Press, Inc.
A Highlights Company
815 Church Street
Honesdale, Pennsylvania 18431
Printed in Mexico

Publisher Cataloging-in-Publication Data
Harrison, David L.
   The animals' song / by David L. Harrison ; illustrated by Chris L. Demarest.—1st ed.
[32]p. : col.ill. ; cm.
Summary : A picture book in rhyme featuring animals joining a dance one by one.
ISBN 1-56397-144-5
1. Animals—Fiction—Juvenile literature. 2. Stories in rhyme—Juvenile literature. [1.
Animals—Fiction. 2. Stories in rhyme.] I. Demarest, Chris L., ill. II. Title.
   [E]—dc20   1997   AC   CIP
Library of Congress Catalog Card Number 93-74138

First edition, 1997
Book designed by Tim Gillner
The text of this book is set in 20-point Melior.
The illustrations are done in watercolors and pen and ink.

10 9 8 7 6 5 4 3 2 1